Marty Aardvark

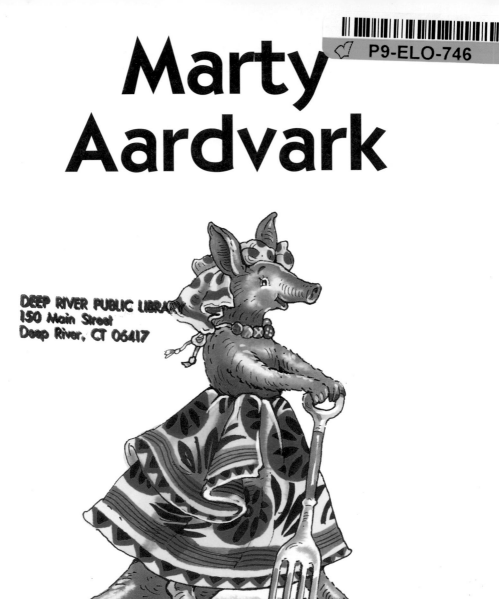

Barbara deRubertis
Illustrated by Eva Vagreti Cockrille

The Kane Press
New York

Cover Design: Sheryl Kagen

Library of Congress Cataloging-in-Publication Data

DeRubertis, Barbara.
Marty Aardvark/Barbara deRubertis; illustrated by Eva Vagreti Cockrille.
p. cm.
"A let's read together book."

Summary: An aardvark who longs to travel far takes a trip downriver on a barge and has quite an adventurous journey, before deciding that she will be glad to return home to her ant farm.
ISBN 1-57565-042-8 (pbk.: alk. paper)
[1. Aardvark--Fiction. 2. Voyages and travels--Fiction. 3. Stories in rhyme.] I. Vagreti Cockrille, Eva, ill. II. Title.
PZ8.3.D455Mar 1998
[E]--dc21   97-44312
                                                    CIP
                                                    AC

10 9 8 7 6 5 4 3 2 1

First published in the United States of America in 1998 by The Kane Press.
Printed in Hong Kong.

LET'S READ TOGETHER is a trademark of The Kane Press.

Marty Aardvark
works so hard.
She cares for both
her farm and yard.

3

Marty works
from dawn till dark.
Her farm and yard
look like a park.

SUPER
GROW

But when she sees
a wishing star,
she wishes she
could travel far.

Marty wants
to ride a barge,
a river barge
that's not *too* large.

She'll ride the barge
down to the sea.
The *sea* is where
she wants to be.

She'll board a ship.
And while she sails,
she might see marlins,
sharks, or whales!

She's saved enough
to travel far.
The money's in
her cookie jar.

So Marty Aardvark
takes her jar
and marches out
to start her car.

Cookie Jar

Marty drives
her car to town.
She parks. And then
she looks around.

A charming sign says,
"Travel Smart
with Parker Lark."
Good place to start!

Marty talks with
Parker Lark.
She asks, "How soon
can I depart?"

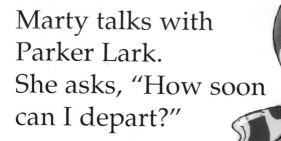

Parker Lark says,
"Right away!
Marty, you can
leave today!

"The river barge
departs at noon.
The captain will
start boarding soon."

13

Marty hurries
to the wharf.
She waves to Parker
with her scarf.

The ride is smooth.
They glide along
as Captain Sparky
sings a song.

He sings and plays
an old guitar.
He sings of rivers
near and far.

When Marty sees
the salty sea,
she says, "That's where
I want to be.

"A ship will take
me out to sea.
Oh, there will be
so much to see!"

Captain Sparky
docks the barge.
Marty finds her
ship. It's large!

The ship departs.
And all goes well.
Then Marty hears
the warning bell!

A storm blows in.
The sky grows dark.
The rain pours down.
Is that a shark?

"Hark!" the skipper
cries. "Beware!
There's danger in
the air. Take care!"

Marty Aardvark
grips the rail.
But then she slips,
head over tail!

No one sees
poor Marty fall.
No one hears
poor Marty call . . .

until a marlin
comes her way.
And Starla Marlin
saves the day!

Starla says,
"Hop on my back!
I see a shark.
It might attack."

The shark just plays.
It dips and darts.
But Starla arcs
and then departs.

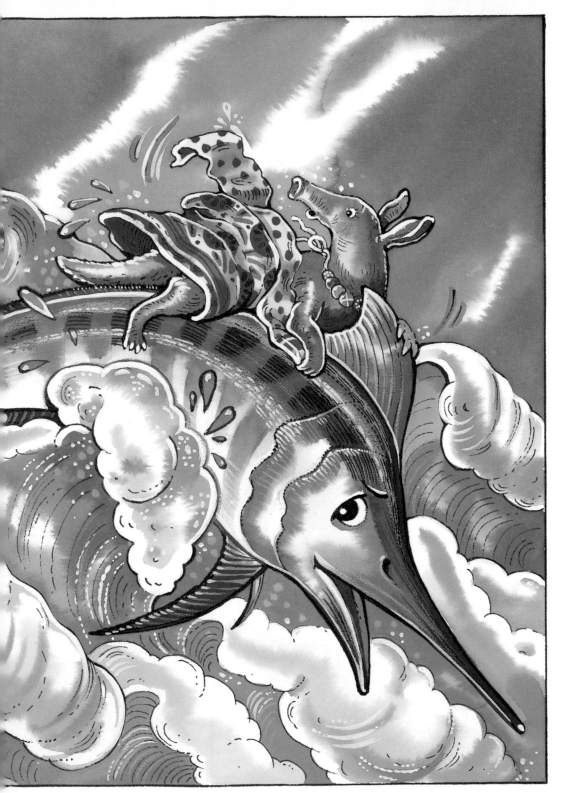

The shark is gone.
The storm has passed.
The stars are out.
It's calm at last.

Starla Marlin
swims all night
until the barge
comes into sight.

Starla stops
beside the wharf.
Then Marty waves
her soggy scarf.

She calls, "You saved
my life, my friend!"
as Starla swims
around the bend.

When Marty climbs
aboard the barge,
Captain Sparky's
smile is large.

Sparky sings.
The air is warm.
And Marty thinks
about her farm.

"I saw the river
and the sea.
Now home is where
I want to be . . . ."

That is, until
my cookie jar
is full again!
Then I'll go FAR!"